# The Little Train

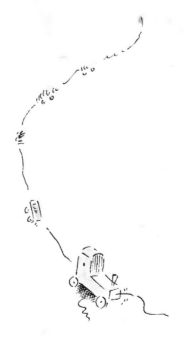

by JUDY HINDLEY

illustrated by ROBERT KENDALL

Orchard Books · New York

Orchard Books, A division of Franklin Watts, Inc.
387 Park Avenue South, New York, NY 10016

Manufactured in the United States of America. Printed by General Offset
Co., Inc. Bound by Horowitz/Rae. Book design by Mina Greenstein.
The text of this book is set in 14 pt. Bembo. The illustrations are
pen and ink and watercolor, reproduced in four colors.
10  9  8  7  6  5  4  3  2  1
Library of Congress Cataloging-in-Publication Data
Hindley, Judy. The little train / story by Judy Hindley : pictures by
Robert Kendall. — 1st American ed.   p.   cm.
Summary: A tiny wooden train is made by a craftsman and acquired
by a small boy.
ISBN 0-531-05850-6.   ISBN 0-531-08450-7 (lib. bdg.)
[1. Railroads—Trains—Fiction.  2. Toys—Fiction.  3. Woodwork—
Fiction.]  I. Kendall, Robert, date. ill.  II. Title.
PZ7.H5696Li  1990  [E]—dc20  89-35385  CIP  AC

For finders
and seekers

Once upon a time
there was a train.
It's in this picture,
you just can't see it yet.
It is a very small train.
Its engine is not much bigger
than your hand.
Its cars are not much longer
than your finger.
And its wheels
are as small as buttons.

But besides,
the train is hidden.
It is still inside the
timber of its tree—
one of these trees
that rise above
the riverbank.

Here is the man
who came
to cut the tree down . . .

and took it
to the mill
to be sawed up.

Here are the men
who built a house
with most of it. . . .

And here is Ben,
who found the bits left over—
the chunks and scraps
in which
the train is waiting.

High in this building,
way above the real trains
in the railway yard,
Ben is at work.
It is late at night,
but he's awake—
working at his bench
all alone.

The soft light
lower down
is a night-light.
This is where a little boy
is sleeping.
During the day
he loves to watch the trains.
Even in his dreams
he sees them running . . .

engines and boxcars,
coal cars and flatbeds
that look as small as toys,
far, far below.

Here is Ben
at work.

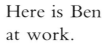

All around
are the things he makes—

breadboards and bookends,
doorstops and wooden spoons.

But tonight
he cannot work
on things like this.

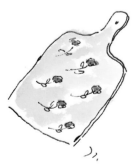

 Is this a doorstop?

No.

 Is it a bookend?

No.

What can it be?

All night long
Ben works. . . .

And when the dawn comes,
here's the little train.

It could climb
a very little mountain.

It could ford
a very little stream.

All it needs is someone small
to take it there.

It is morning now
and daytime noises have begun.
Down below,
the trains are rumbling.
It's time for Ben
to go to market.
But he turns back
to take just one last look.
When he leaves,
the train is in his bag.

This is the train's
first adventure.
No steep hills
to travel up.
No ravines
to travel down.
Only darkness.

At last the train is in the light again.
But what is this?

Where are the streams and tracks and bridges?

Where is someone small who understands small things?

Here he is.

From now on,
Ben will have more work to do.

The train will need a station
and a bridge.

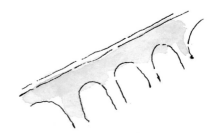

It will need signals
to say when it should stop.

Soon, there will be tiny cars
and tiny houses
on Ben's workbench.

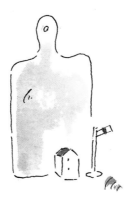

At times the train may be lost
in deep, dark caves,

stranded on lonely mountains,

or left beneath the stars
in desert sands.

Will someone always come
to find this train?

Of course.

Good night, train.

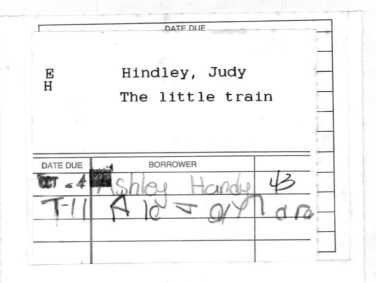

| DATE DUE | | | |
|---|---|---|---|

E H      **Hindley, Judy**

**The little train**

| DATE DUE | BORROWER | | |
|---|---|---|---|
| OCT 4 | Ashley Handy | 43 | |
| T-11 | A 10 4 qy 1 a c | | |

E H      Hindley, Judy

The little train

**Anderson Elementary**

 GUMDROP BOOKS - Bethany, Missouri